To David, for making all of this possible

Note to Parents

THE REAL MOTHER GOOSE ABCs is not just for children beginning to learn their alphabet. With the classic Mother Goose rhymes on each page, it's also a wonderful book for older children with basic reading skills already in place. As a read-aloud book, they can have the joy of learning these classic rhymes while enriching their alphabet skills.

And for all ages, there's the search and discover fun of poring over beautiful full-color illustrations, each of which has several objects beginning with a particular letter of the alphabet for children to find on their own.

THE REAL
MOTHER
GOOSE
ABCs

Illustrated by
Patty McCloskey-Padgett

CHECKERBOARD PRESS

NEW YORK

Aa

APPLE

OH, DEAR!

Dear, dear! what can the matter be?
Two old women got up in an apple-
tree;
One came down, and the other
stayed till Saturday.

BLACK SHEEP

BAA, BAA, BLACK SHEEP

Baa, baa, black sheep,
Have you any wool?
Yes, marry, have I,
Three bags full;

One for my master,
One for my dame,
But none for the little boy
Who cries in the lane.

Cc

CURLY-LOCKS

Curly-locks, Curly-locks, wilt thou be mine?
Thou shalt not wash the dishes, nor yet feed
the swine;
But sit on a cushion, and sew a fine seam
And feed upon strawberries, sugar, and
cream.

DOLLAR

Dd

THE TEN O'CLOCK SCHOLAR

A diller, a dollar, a ten o'clock scholar!
What makes you come so soon?
You used to come at ten o'clock,
But now you come at noon.

ELIZABETH

Elizabeth, Elspeth, Betsy, and
    Bess,
They all went together to seek a
    bird's nest;
They found a bird's nest with five
    eggs in,
They all took one, and left four in.

FIDDLE

F f

THE CAT AND THE FIDDLE

Hey, diddle, diddle!
　　The cat and the fiddle,
The cow jumped over the moon;
　　The little dog laughed
　　To see such sport,
And the dish ran away with the spoon.

Gg

GARDEN

MARY, MARY, QUITE CONTRARY

Mary, Mary, quite contrary,
    How does your garden grow?
Silver bells and cockle-shells,
    And pretty maids all of a row.

HOBBY-HORSE

THE HOBBY-HORSE

I had a little hobby-horse,
    And it was dapple gray;
Its head was made of pea-straw,
    Its tail was made of hay.

I sold it to an old woman
    For a copper groat;
And I'll not sing my song again
    Without another coat.

Ii

ICICLE

AN ICICLE

Lives in winter,
Dies in summer,
And grows with its roots upward!

JACK

Jj

Jack be nimble, Jack be quick,
Jack jump over the candle-stick.

Kk

KING

LITTLE KING BOGGEN

Little King Boggen, he built a fine hall,
Pie-crust and pastry-crust, that was the wall;
The windows were made of black puddings and white,
And slated with pan-cakes,—you ne'er saw the like!

LITTLE BOY BLUE

Little Boy Blue, come, blow your
   horn!
The sheep's in the meadow, the
   cow's in the corn.
Where's the little boy that looks
   after the sheep?
Under the haystack, fast asleep!

Mm

MAID

MY MAID MARY

My maid Mary she minds the dairy,
While I go a-hoeing and mowing
each morn;

Gaily run the reel and the little
spinning wheel.
While I am singing and mowing
my corn.

NANCY

NANCY DAWSON

Nancy Dawson was so fine
She wouldn't get up to serve the
    swine;
She lies in bed till eight or
    nine,
So it's Oh, poor Nancy Dawson.

And do ye ken Nancy Dawson,
    honey?
The wife who sells the barley, honey?
She won't get up to feed her swine,
And do ye ken Nancy Dawson,
    honey?

Oo OLD

OLD MOTHER HUBBARD

Old Mother Hubbard
Went to the cupboard,
    To give her poor dog a bone;
But when she got there
    The cupboard was bare,
    And so the poor dog had none.

PLUM

Pp

LITTLE JACK HORNER

Little Jack Horner
Sat in the corner,
    Eating of Christmas pie:
He put in his thumb,
And pulled out a plum,
    And said, "What a good boy
    am I!"

QUEEN

Qq

THE TARTS

The Queen of Hearts,
      She made some tarts,
All on a summer's day;
      The Knave of Hearts,
      He stole the tarts,
And took them clean away.

Rr

ROBIN REDBREAST

Little Robin Redbreast sat upon a tree,
Up went Pussy-Cat, down went he,
Down came Pussy-Cat, away Robin
	ran,
Says little Robin Redbreast: "Catch
	me if you can!"

Ss

SPIDER

TUFFET

Tt

MISS MUFFET

Little Miss Muffet
Sat on a tuffet,
Eating of curds and whey;
There came a big spider,
And sat down beside her,
And frightened Miss Muffet away.

Uu

UNICORN

THE LION AND THE UNICORN

The Lion and the Unicorn were
  fighting for the crown,
The Lion beat the Unicorn all
  around the town.

Some gave them white bread, and
  some gave them brown,
Some gave them plum-cake, and
  sent them out of town.

VELVET

Vv

HARK! HARK!

Hark, hark! the dogs do bark!
　　Beggars are coming to town:
Some in jags, and some in rags,
　　And some in velvet gown.

Ww

WILLIE

WEE WILLIE WINKIE

Wee Willie Winkie runs through the town,
Upstairs and downstairs, in his nightgown;

Rapping at the window, crying through the lock,
"Are the children in their beds? Now it's eight o'clock."

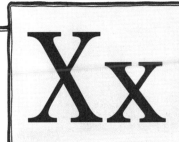

X x x

HOT-CROSS BUNS

Hot-cross Buns!
 Hot-cross Buns!
One a penny, two a penny,
 Hot-cross Buns!
 Hot-cross Buns!
 Hot-cross Buns!
If ye have no daughters,
Give them to your sons.

You

FOR BABY

You shall have an apple,
YOU shall have a plum,
You shall have a rattle,
When papa comes home.

Zz

ZZZ

SLEEP, BABY, SLEEP

Sleep, baby, sleep,
Our cottage vale is deep:
The little lamb is on the green,
With woolly fleece so soft and clean—
Sleep, baby, sleep.

ANSWERS

Aa: animals, ankles, apples, apron, arms, ax

Bb: bags, balloon, barrel, basket, birdhouse, birds, black sheep, boy

Cc: cage, canary, cap, cat, chair, chin, cream, creamer, curls, Curly-Locks

Dd: desk, dog, door, doorknob, doormat, dunce cap

Ee: ear, eggs, elbows, Elizabeth, eyebrows, eyelashes, eyes

Ff: feather, feet, fiddle, fingers, frill collar, frog, fur

Gg: garden, gate, girls, gloves, goose, grass

Hh: hair, hands, hats, haystacks, heads, heart, heels (of shoes), hobby-horse

Ii: ice, ice-cream cone, ice skates, icicles, igloo

Jj: Jack, jack-in-the-box, jacks, jam, jars, jelly, jug

Kk: keyhole, King Boggen, kite, kitties, knobs, knuckles

Ll: ladder, lamb, leaves, legs, lips, Little Boy Blue, lollipop

Mm: maid Mary, mice, milk, mop, mountains, mouth

Nn: nail, Nancy Dawson, necks, nest, nightcap, nightgown, nose

Oo: Old Mother Hubbard, open (cupboard), oval (window), oven

Pp: pan, pie, pillow, pitcher, plate, plum

Qq: Queen of Hearts, quill pen, quilt, quiver (container holding arrows), quivers (arrows)

Rr: rabbits, road, Robin Redbreast, rocks, roof, rooster, roots

Ss: sheep, shelf, shoes, shoulder, socks, soldier, spider, spiderweb, spoons, stool, sugar bowl

Tt: table, teakettle, thumb, top hat, toy box, toys, tuffet

Uu: umbrella, unicorn, unicycle, uniforms

Vv: vegetables, velvet (gown), vest, violin

Ww: walls, web, Wee Willie Winkie, well, wheel, wheelbarrow, windows, windowsill, wood

Xx: x's (in buns), x's (in pants), xylophone

Yy: yams, yard, yarn, yo-yo

Zz: z's (from sleeping baby), zebra, zigzag (on footstool)